Far-Fetched Pets

YOUR
PET BEAR

By Bobbie Hamsa

Illustrations by Tom Dunnington

Consultant:
Roger E. Chudzik
Bear keeper
Lincoln Park Zoo, Chicago

CHILDRENS PRESS®

CHICAGO

CAUTION
Far-fetched pets should not be kept in your house or apart-
ment or yard. Don't ask for one for your birthday or
Christmas. Go to the zoo or visit the library. There you can
learn more about your favorite far-fetched pet.

Library of Congress Cataloging in Publication Data

Hamsa, Bobbi.
    Your pet bear.

    (Far-fetched pets)
    SUMMARY: Discusses the advantages of having a
bear for a pet, such as his ability to dig a good
hole and eat all the foods that one hates, and gives
instructions for his general care and housing.
    [1. Bears—Anecdotes, facetiae, satire, etc.]
I. Dunnington, Tom. II. Title. III. Series.
PZ7.H1887Yn   [E]   79-24938
ISBN 0-516-04481-8

This is a bear.

An American Black Bear.

He is not always black.

He comes in different shades of yellow and brown.

Pretend that he is your pet.

He has thick, shaggy fur.
Big, sharp teeth.
Bigger, sharper claws.

Thockmorton? Neru? Shaggy? Fred?

Adolph? King?

Bob?

And almost no tail at all.
What will you name your pet bear?

5

Menu
• MouseMuffin
• Fly Fricasee
• Pine Cone Pie
• Buggy Pudding
• Grass Goulasch
• Carrot Crunch

6

CARE AND FEEDING OF YOUR PET

Bears eat EVERYTHING.

Fruits, vegetables, bugs, leaves, grass, and mice.

Even pinecones and clam shells if they're really hungry.

For a treat, have mom fix squirrel
stuffed with carrots and covered
with honey gravy.
But don't let him eat too much.
Squirrel is very fattening.

Once every year or so you'll want
to groom your pet.
This is very simple.

Cover him with mud.
Let it dry.

Then let him scratch it off.
This gets rid of old fur.
And new fleas.
It also helps take some of the
stink off.

Your bear will need a quiet place
to sleep.
A cave is best.
Or a basement.
Or perhaps you have a hollow tree?

He could sleep with you, but he's
a very messy roommate.

Besides, it might make your teddy
jealous.

If your bear is young, he's smaller than you are.

But in two short years, he'll be as tall as your dad.

Think about where you will put your bear.

Your bear can't see or hear very
well.

So don't bother taking him to
movies.

And say "no" when he asks to drive.

Two things really scare your bear.
Porcupines.
And quicksand.
So before he moves in, hide your
mother's pincushion.
And ask dad to drain the swamp.

Play with your bear.
He likes tag.
And tumbling.
But his favorite game is "Hide
'N' Seek" (because he finds you
every time).

Take him to the river.
He dearly loves to swim.
No one's better at catching fish—
and he doesn't even need a pole.

20

One final thing . . .
your bear loves to travel.

He has lots of cousins in
Yellowstone Park.

So if you go, take him along for
a visit.

TRAINING

With a little training, your bear
can be very useful.

He can dig a dandy hole . . .
     give your friends some wild
     "bear-back" rides . . .

sniff out Mom's hiding places for
candy and gum . . .
hug Aunt Gertrude *for* you.

He'll eat all the foods you hate . . .
scratch itchy places on your back . . .
and make the scariest monster
on Halloween.

Best of all, your bear can make
your brother do W-H-A-T-E-V-E-R you
want him to!

Your bear is a pretty good climber.

So he can put baby birds back up in trees . . . or bring frightened kittens down.

He can hang Christmas lights around the house . . . and reach the tip-top kitchen cupboard.

If you get lost in the forest, your bear will find food. Nuts. Berries. And other wild things. He may even share with you.

These are only a few of the things your pet can do.

Can you think of more?

If you take good care of him, your bear will live maybe 25 years.

And he'll be the best pet you ever had.

Facts about your pet American Black Bear (Euarctos americanus)

Size at birth: 10 to 14 inches long (25.4 to 35.6 cm);
12 to 18 ounces (340 to 510 grams)

Number of newborn: 1 to 4, two are very common

Average size when grown: males are about 6 feet (1.83 m) when standing on their hind legs, weigh about 400 pounds (181 kg)

Type of food eaten: mostly roots, berries, and leaves. They will eat fish and sometimes carrion (dead animals).

Expected lifespan: 15 to 25 years

Names—male: boar or he-bear
female: sow, she-bear, or dam
young: cub
group: Bears are most commonly found as solitary animals.
Bears form in groups mostly around garbage dumps.

Where found: Large tracts of wooded areas of North America, north of central Mexico.

About the Author

Bobbie Hamsa was born and raised in Nebraska. She was graduated from the University of Nebraska in Lincoln with a B.A. in English and zoology.

During the course of her life she has pursued many careers including a ten-year stint as copywriter for Bozell, Inc., an advertising and public relations firm in Omaha. For seven years she wrote and produced print, point-of-sale, radio, and television commercials for Mutual of Omaha's Wild Kingdom, the Emmy-award winning wildlife series starring Marlin Perkins and Jim Fowler.

After owning and running a deli in Sonoma, California, she is now back in the Midwest in pursuit of a nursing career. She splits her time between Grand Island, Nebraska, where her parents, Dr. and Mrs. R.A. Hamsa, reside.

Bobbie is divorced and the parent of a son, John, a recent graduate of the California Culinary Academy.

About the Artist

Tom Dunnington has his home and studio in Oak Park, Illinois. He divides his time between illustrating books for children, painting wildlife subjects, working with young people in the community, and being a card-carrying "grampa" for his seven wonderful grandchildren. Tom has done many books for Childrens Press and considers himself a most fortunate man because his work is fun.